Sparks of Temptation

A Small-Town Romance Where Forced Proximity Sparks Passion Between a Protective Firefighter and a Stubborn Chef

Hana York

Pink Pop Publishing

Sparks of Temptation

(Hearts on Duty Book 1)

Copyright © 2025 by Hana York

All rights reserved.

www.HanaYork.com

Contents

Chapter One

♥

OLIVIA

The smell of burnt sugar hit me a second before the fire alarm started screaming like a furious banshee.

"Oh, come on, it's just a little smoke," I muttered, grabbing a towel and frantically waving it at the alarm.

Meanwhile, flames curled mockingly from the pan on my stovetop, ignoring my attempt to smother them with a pot lid.

"This is fine. Totally manageable," I lied—mostly to myself.

Biscuit gave me a long, unimpressed stare from his perch on a stool before bolting out of the kitchen. Traitor.

I spun toward the pantry, reaching for the fire extinguisher—except... it wasn't there.

My stomach dropped.

Oh, for the love of—

Right. The Great Breakup Item Grab. My ex took my cast-iron skillet, my favorite coffee mug, and apparently, my damn fire extinguisher when he left six months ago.

The pounding on my front door nearly made me drop the spatula I had no memory of holding.

"Fire department! Open up!"

Oh, fantastic.

I coughed against the smoke, stumbling toward the door. "Coming!"

When I yanked it open, the man on my porch was alarmingly attractive.

Tall. Broad. Covered in enough turnout gear to make my already overheated body seem ten degrees warmer. His helmet shadowed most of his face, but those sharp blue eyes locked onto mine with laser focus.

And just like that, the fire wasn't the only thing setting me on edge.

"Ma'am, are you the only one inside?"

The firefighter's voice was all business, but I barely processed the question over the chaos in my kitchen.

"Yes, but—"

"Any pets?"

"Just Biscuit—he's fine."

Before I could add that my cat was likely filing an official complaint against me, the firefighter brushed past, barking orders into his radio. Two more firefighters followed, moving efficiently as smoke curled toward the ceiling.

I stood there, blinking, as my kitchen became a full-blown emergency scene.

By the time the flames were out, my once-cozy kitchen looked like it had lost a bar fight. Soot streaked the countertops, the smell of charred sugar clung to the air, and my beloved copper pots hung at drunken angles, as if mocking me for my life choices.

The first firefighter, Mr. Tall, Broad, and Authority Complex—pulled off his helmet, ruffling a hand through tousled dark hair.

He had a strong jawline, sharp blue eyes, and a smirk that made my palm itch to smack it.

Or, alternatively, kiss it. But I was obviously suffering from smoke inhalation.

"I think we're good," he said, tone light like my kitchen hadn't just survived a culinary apocalypse.

I planted my hands on my hips. "Define 'good'." I motioned to the wreckage.

He chuckled, the sound low and way too compelling for someone who had just seen me at my most unhinged. "It's not burnt to the ground. I call that a win."

I huffed. "Well, thanks for your heroic efforts, but I had it under control."

His eyebrows shot up. "Really?" His gaze dropped to the charred remains of my dish towel. "Because it looked like Biscuit was about to call 911 himself."

I crossed my arms, glaring. "I don't need commentary from someone who doesn't know the difference between a controlled flame and an actual emergency."

"Controlled flame?" He cocked his head and gestured to the blackened pan on the stove. "That's what you're calling it?"

"Yes," I said, standing my ground. "It was supposed to be crème brûlée."

"Ah." His smirk widened as he took a step back. "I see the problem. Crème brûlée should end with a torch, not start with one."

I opened my mouth—probably to insult him—but for some infuriating reason, my traitorous lips twitched.

Damn it.

I glared at the smirking firefighter, my pulse racing for reasons I wasn't about to examine too closely.

"Thanks for the cooking tips, Chef Hotshot. Should I expect a bill for your professional advice?"

"Only if you want more of it." His grin widened. "Sarcasm's extra."

I narrowed my eyes as he leaned too casually against the counter, making zero effort to leave. Surely his crew would call him away any second now, back to... I don't know, firefighter things. But when I glanced toward the doorway, the others were already packing up and heading out—leaving me alone with Mr. Smirky.

Great.

"I didn't catch your name," I said, mostly out of politeness. Definitely not because my brain was curious about anything beyond how fast he could get out of my house.

"Jack Lawson," he said, extending a soot-streaked hand.

I hesitated before taking it, immediately regretting the decision. His grip was warm, steady, strong—and the teasing in his blue eyes softened into something else for a split second.

Something dangerous.

A tiny, unwelcome flutter spread through my chest, and I pulled my hand back far too quickly.

"Well, Jack Lawson, thanks for the assist." My tone snapped back to sharp. "I'll take it from here."

Jack didn't move. "Are you sure? I could stick around and help with the cleanup. Make sure you don't light any more pans on fire."

I bristled, grabbing a sponge and scrubbing at the counter—only to smear the soot around making it worse. Fantastic.

"I can handle it," I muttered.

Jack watched me for a beat, then smirked, again. "You're not great at accepting help, are you?"

I froze mid-scrub. Slowly, I turned to glare at him.

"I'm great at accepting help when it's necessary."

"Right." His grin widened.

My jaw tightened. "Look, I've had a day, okay? And I don't need a firefighter slash comedian making it worse."

Jack raised his hands in mock surrender. "Fair enough. But for the record, your day could've been much worse, so maybe it's not as bad as you think."

I wanted to argue. Truly. But something about his tone made me hesitate.

"Thanks," I said begrudgingly. "For not letting my day end with a pile of ashes."

Jack's expression softened, the teasing edge dimming slightly as a genuine smile tugged at his lips. "Anytime."

Before I could figure out how to respond, Biscuit sauntered back into the kitchen, meowing dramatically as if emerging from the wreckage of battle.

Jack crouched, holding out a hand. "This Biscuit?"

"Yep." I rolled my eyes. "He's fine, by the way. Didn't even look back as he ran for his life."

Jack chuckled, scratching behind Biscuit's ears. "Smart cat. Knows when to get out of the heat."

I exhaled. "That makes one of us."

Jack stood, giving Biscuit one last pat before turning to me. "I'll leave you to your... crème brûlée revival project. But you need an extinguisher." He raised an eyebrow. "Maybe pick one up before your next experiment."

I bristled, already reaching for a comeback, but before I could fire off a well-earned retort, he was walking toward the door, his boots heavy against the tile.

At the last second, he glanced over his shoulder, grin firmly in place.

"See you around, Olivia."

The door clicked shut, leaving me standing in the middle of my wrecked kitchen, soot-covered sponge in one hand and my traitorous heart thudding entirely too hard in my chest.

***

JACK

I shut Olivia's front door behind me and took a long, steady breath. Damn.

I'd walked into that house expecting a standard call—small kitchen fire, quick fix, maybe a grateful smile, and a "thank you" before returning to the station. What I hadn't expected was Olivia Harper.

Stubborn. Sharp-tongued. Utterly uninterested in my presence.

And, hell, was she gorgeous.

I removed my gloves, shoving them into my back pocket as I descended the porch steps. The smell of smoke still clung to my gear, but underneath it, I could still catch the faint scent of vanilla and something sweet—something distinctly Olivia.

The woman had been two seconds away from burning her kitchen down, and instead of relief, she'd given me attitude. Like I was inconveniencing her by saving her house.

I should be annoyed. And I was. Kind of. But mostly, I was intrigued.

Because Olivia Harper wasn't like anyone else in Anchor Bay.

I climbed into my truck, gripping the steering wheel tighter than necessary. I'd met plenty of people who didn't like taking help—myself included—but Olivia? She took it to a whole new level. She had something to prove, and I couldn't help but wonder to whom.

Or why.

The radio crackled, snapping me out of my thoughts.

"Lawson, you clear from the scene?"

I grabbed the radio. "Yeah, fire's out. Just some kitchen damage. No injuries." Unless you counted Olivia's bruised ego.

"Copy that."

I set the radio back in place but didn't start the truck immediately. Instead, I glanced back at Olivia's house. She was in there right now—probably grumbling to her cat about me while scrubbing soot off her countertops.

I shook my head, a reluctant grin pulling at my lips.

Yeah. Olivia Harper was going to be trouble.

And for some damn reason, I was already looking forward to it.

Chapter Two

♥

OLIVIA

Several days later, I was elbow-deep in pantry organization when I heard Mrs. Barlow's familiar shuffle on the porch. Before I could even call out, the door swung open. Because, of course, knocking wasn't her style.

"Hello, my dear!" she chirped, humming as she crossed the threshold with the confidence of someone who'd done it a hundred times before.

I sighed, already knowing where this was headed. Mrs. Barlow didn't do casual visits. "Hi, Mrs. Barlow. What brings you by?"

"Oh, just passing through," she said breezily, setting a covered dish on the counter with a satisfied pat. "Thought you might need some lasagna. You're starting to look like a beanpole, dear."

I glanced between the casserole and my reflection in the toaster. Pretty sure I looked exactly the same as yesterday, but I wasn't about to argue with a woman who considered butter an essential food group. "I'm fine. Thanks."

"Well, you're about to be finer," she said with a knowing smile. "You remember Jack Lawson, don't you?"

I froze, my hand gripping a jar of flour. A rush of heat crept up my neck before I could stop it. "The firefighter who came when my kitchen caught fire? Yeah, he's hard to forget."

Mrs. Barlow leaned in like she was about to share the town's juiciest secret. "Poor boy's apartment flooded this week—completely uninhabitable! I told him you've got that darling little guesthouse out back. Seemed like the perfect solution."

I stared at her. "You what?"

"I told him to stop by and talk to you about it," she repeated, as if she hadn't just steamrolled over my personal space and decision-making in one fell swoop. "He's such a nice young man, don't you think? And single!"

I pinched the bridge of my nose. "Mrs. Barlow, I don't—"

"Don't thank me, dear. It's what neighbors are for." She patted my cheek like I was a fussy toddler before turning toward the door. "He should be stopping by later, so do try to be polite."

"Mrs. Barlow—"

"Oh, and enjoy the lasagna! It's my special recipe."

In a blink, she vanished, leaving me frozen in place like an idiot in my own kitchen.

I exhaled slowly, my eyes fixed on the door she'd made sure to shut on her way out.

A houseguest. Jack Lawson.

For the love of all things holy.

***

When the doorbell rang a short while later, I sighed, wiping my hands on a dish towel. I had two choices—hide in the pantry until Jack gave up or face this head-on.

Grumbling under my breath, I swung the door open.

Jack stood on my porch, duffel bag slung over one shoulder and an easy smile playing on his lips.

And, oh, wow.

Without the bulky firefighting gear, he was distractingly solid. Strong. The kind of man built to carry people out of burning buildings—which he literally did, Olivia, get a grip.

His gray t-shirt clung to broad shoulders and a chest that made my fingers twitch. His faded jeans sat low on his hips, and as my traitorous gaze dipped lower, I caught the briefest glimpse of skin where his shirt had ridden up.

I jerked my attention back to his face. Eyes up, Harper.

"Hey there," Jack said, his voice warm, laced with amusement. "Mrs. Barlow said you might have a place for me to crash?"

I blinked. "Uh, yeah. About that..."

My words trailed off as he shifted, his blue eyes crinkling at the corners, that damn smile still firmly in place.

"Bad time? I can come back later if you want."

"No, it's fine," I said quickly, forcing a breath into my lungs. "Just wasn't expecting you so soon, that's all." I stepped back, motioning inside. "Come in, might as well get this over with."

Because nothing said "good decision-making," like letting the man who already threw me off my game move into my backyard.

What could possibly go wrong?

Jack stepped inside, glancing around my living room with an easy grin. "Nice place. Much cozier without all the smoke."

I rolled my eyes, but damn it, the corner of my mouth twitched. "Very funny. I'll have you know I haven't set anything on fire since then."

Jack chuckled, the sound warm and teasing. "That's a relief. I was starting to think saving you might become a full-time job—not that I'd mind."

I ignored how that comment sent a ridiculous flutter through my chest and cleared my throat. "So, Mrs. Barlow mentioned you needed a place to stay?"

Jack nodded, running a hand through his already messy dark hair. My eyes betrayed me by following the flex of his arm because, of course, they did. "Yeah, my apartment flooded. Burst pipe. It's going to take weeks to fix all the damage."

"That's rough." I folded my arms, mostly so I wouldn't be tempted to rub the back of my suddenly warm neck. "Sorry to hear that."

"Thanks," Jack said, his gaze flicking over my face, pausing briefly at my mouth. His eyes darkened slightly before meeting mine again, and I suddenly forgot how to stand like a normal human.

I needed to get him out of my house before I did something mortifying, like trip over my own feet or openly stare at his forearms again.

"I do have a guesthouse," I admitted, forcing my voice to sound completely unaffected. "It's small, but it has the basics—bed, bathroom, kitchenette."

Jack's face lit up like I'd just handed him a winning lottery ticket. "That sounds perfect. Anything is better than a bunk at the station. I promise I won't be any trouble."

I hesitated. Jack might not be trouble, but my own ability to ignore him? That was another story.

"It's out back," I said finally, waving toward the door. "I'll show you."

I guided him from the kitchen into the garden, conscious of his steps trailing mine. Golden late-day sun washed over the space, catching on the herbs and flowers.

"Impressive," Jack said, eyeing the neat rows.

"Just figuring it out as I go," I said with a shrug. "But thanks."

The guesthouse sat at the garden's edge, a small cottage that looked like it belonged in a fairytale. I wrestled briefly with the stubborn lock, hyper-aware of Jack standing close behind me, before finally opening the door.

Jack had to duck slightly to step inside, his broad frame making the space seem smaller. His eyebrows lifted as he took in the room. The sunlight filtering through the sheer curtains cast everything in a soft glow—the sage-green walls, the butcher-block counter, the handmade quilt draped over the bed in ocean blues and forest greens.

"This is incredible," Jack murmured, dropping his duffel bag to the floor with a thud. His fingers brushed over the kitchen countertop, and something warm flickered in my chest—pride, maybe.

I'd spent months fixing up this place. Weekends covered in sawdust, swearing at video tutorials, debating paint colors. And now it was getting some actual use.

I nodded toward the bathroom. "It's all yours. Fair warning—the shower needs some sweet-talking. Just wiggle the handle, and you'll be fine."

Jack grinned. "Got it. Charm the plumbing. Anything else I should know?"

"No, I don't think so. I'll let you get settled in."

I turned to go, but Jack's fingers circled my wrist before I could reach the door. His touch was warm and solid and sent a jolt of something unwelcome straight to my stomach.

"Olivia."

The way he said my name—low, sincere—made my throat dry.

"I really can't thank you enough."

I waved him off, forcing a casual smile. "It's nothing. Happy to help."

Jack ran a hand through his hair again, and I resisted groaning. How many times can one man run his fingers through his hair before it becomes a public hazard?

"I promise I won't be a bother," he said, his voice quieter. "You won't even know I'm here."

I swallowed hard. "Okay, well... I'll, um, leave you to it."

The words tumbled out too fast, too awkwardly, and I wanted to kick myself. I offered a tight smile before practically fleeing, closing the door behind me.

Only once I was back inside my house, safe from the unsettling pull of Jack Lawson, did I let out a breath.

This was fine. Totally fine.

I just had to survive however long it took for his apartment to get fixed.

No problem at all.

***

JACK

I let out a slow breath as the door clicked shut behind Olivia. I scrubbed a hand over my face and took a good look around. The place was impressive—cozy but thoughtfully put together, with the kind of little details that made a space feel like a home. The soft quilt on the bed, the worn wood floors, the sage-green walls—it was a hell of a lot nicer than my busted apartment or a bunk at the firehouse. But as nice as the guesthouse was, it wasn't what had my pulse still running a little too fast.

That would be Olivia.

The way her green eyes had sparked when she showed me around, that little wrinkle between her brows as she fought with the stubborn lock—like sheer willpower alone would make it cooperate. And then there was that smile, the one she tried to hide but couldn't quite manage.

She was something else. Sharp-witted, stubborn, and so damn beautiful it was distracting.

I sat on the edge of the bed, exhaling hard. I'd barely been here five minutes, and already I felt like trouble was brewing. Not the kind that landed you in a burning building—but the type that snuck up on you, quiet and insistent, until it was too late to turn back.

I hadn't expected to be drawn to her so fast. Yeah, I'd been intrigued when we met—who wouldn't be? She'd stood there in a smoke-filled kitchen, covered in soot, hands on her hips, looking at me like she was ready to take me on in a fight. And now? Now she was letting me stay here, utterly unaware that just being around her was messing with my head.

Hell, I could picture it too easily. Olivia in her kitchen, moving effortlessly as she prepped a meal. The scent of something sweet mixed with the warm vanilla of her shampoo. Me stepping in behind her, close enough to feel her against me, my hands settling at her waist.

She would lean back into me, tilting her head so that the exquisite line of her neck was revealed, and I'd plant gentle kisses from her shoulder up to her ear, breathing in the heady aroma of her floral perfume. In my daydream, Olivia turned to face me, her green eyes heavy-lidded and full of desire. I envisioned lifting her onto the counter and settling between her legs as they wrapped around me, our kisses growing deeper and more desperate with every moment. The vivid daydream left me breathless, and my body reacted instantly.

I shook my head, pushing the thought away before it could go further.

This was a bad idea.

She was doing me a favor, nothing more. And I wasn't about to make things uncomfortable by acting like some guy who couldn't keep his head on straight.

I ran a hand through my hair, forcing my mind to recenter. I just needed to focus. A place to stay, nothing more. No distractions. No overanalyzing the way Olivia's lips curved when she was trying not to smile. No thinking about how her eyes flicked to my mouth when she spoke.

I definitely wasn't reading into that.

"Get it together, Lawson," I muttered, shaking my head.

I stood, rolling my shoulders, trying to loosen the tension in my chest. I needed to keep things simple—respect the space, don't push any boundaries, don't start thinking about what it'd be like to pull Olivia against me and kiss that teasing smirk right off her face.

I cursed under my breath.

Yeah. I was in trouble.

And Olivia Harper? She didn't even know it.

Chapter Three

♥

OLIVIA

The cool morning air was a welcome relief after the lingering smell of smoke in my kitchen. I stepped outside, basket in one hand, scissors in the other, and approached the herb garden. Seeing my plants thriving was a small reassurance that not everything in my life was a disaster.

I crouched near the rosemary, snipping a few sprigs, when movement from the guesthouse porch caught my eye.

And it was then my morning took a sharp turn.

Jack stood against the railing, coffee mug in hand, looking relaxed. Which was fine—except I wasn't mentally prepared for shirtless Jack Lawson before breakfast.

Sunlight caught on his broad shoulders, the muscles in his chest and arms gleaming like he'd stepped out of some rugged firefighter calendar. He looked fresh from a workout, exuding that effortless confidence of someone who had never had an awkward moment.

I immediately looked away.

Not because I was affected. Definitely not. Just a natural reaction. Reflexive eye movement. Totally explainable.

"Morning," Jack called, his voice warm and amused—like he knew exactly what he was doing standing there looking like that.

"Good morning," I managed, focusing very hard on the basil. Basil was safe. Jack was not. I clipped a few more sprigs, added them to my basket, and absolutely did not glance back at the porch. "You're up early."

"Old habit," he said, taking a slow sip of coffee. "Firehouse life. It's hard to sleep when you're used to alarms blaring at random hours."

"Do you have to go into the firehouse today?" The question came out more hopeful than intended, and I winced internally.

Jack grinned. He heard it.

"Nope," he said, stretching like he had all the time in the world. "Got the whole day off."

Of course he did.

"Great," I muttered, straightening with my basket.

Jack smirked over the rim of his coffee. "Why? Trying to get rid of me?"

"No," I said quickly. Too quickly. Damn it. "I just have a lot to do today."

Jack set his mug on the railing, shifting his stance like he was ready for action. "Anything I can help with?"

I blinked. "Come again?"

"You've got a lot to do, right? I'm not great at sitting still, and I'm pretty handy. Anything around here need fixing?" He nodded toward the fence. "That post is wobbling like a drunk sailor. And your gate latch? Pretty sure it's hanging on for dear life."

I hesitated. Not because I didn't need the help but because having Jack here all day would be distracting.

"But isn't this supposed to be your day off?" I ventured.

He shrugged, flashing that easygoing, devastatingly self-assured smile. "Tinkering keeps me sane. Besides, this way, I won't be underfoot while you're working."

I highly doubted that.

Still, getting a few repairs done wouldn't be the worst thing. I let out a slow breath. "Okay. If you're absolutely sure."

Jack was already heading down the steps. "I'll grab my tools. Consider it rent for the guesthouse."

I lingered by the herb garden for a beat longer than necessary, watching him go before shaking myself out of it.

This was fine. Totally fine.

I just needed to focus on my work, not how Jack Lawson looked shirtless.

***

JACK

I crouched near the fence, wrench in hand, tightening the bolts on the loose post. It should have been a simple, straightforward task that kept my hands busy and my mind clear. But my mind was anything but clear.

Because Olivia was inside, and every muffled sound that drifted through the open kitchen window pulled my attention like a magnet.

I could hear her talking—muttering, probably at a recipe that wasn't cooperating. A smile tugged at the corner of my mouth. I could picture her, hands on her hips, glaring down at whatever poor dish had dared to defy her.

I admired that about her—her fire, her determination. Hell, she probably put more passion into making a loaf of bread than most people put into their entire lives. And it was impossible to ignore.

A muscle tightened in my jaw as last night's thoughts tried to creep in—the way my mind had repeatedly drifted to her. My breath hitched at the memory, heat flickering low in my stomach.

"Get a grip, Lawson." I exhaled sharply and tightened another bolt, focusing on the rhythmic pull of muscle instead of how Olivia Harper had burrowed into my brain and refused to leave.

She wasn't interested. That much was obvious. She was polite but distant, always busy, always focused. And even if she were interested? She deserved better than some guy still haunted by his own failures. A guy who, in the quiet moments, still heard the echo of the things he couldn't fix.

I adjusted my grip on the wrench as her voice rang out again, clearer this time.

"You're not supposed to look like that. What am I doing wrong?" A pause. Then, more firmly, "Come on, Olivia. You're better than this."

I bit back a laugh. She was scolding dough, wasn't she?

Shaking my head, I leaned back on my heels. The physical work was good—a distraction. But whatever this pull toward Olivia was, it wasn't exactly productive.

The scent of herbs and fresh soil filled the warm morning air, and I let myself take it in. It was peaceful here. Maybe the most peaceful I'd felt in years.

Then—her voice again, tinged with exasperation.

"Oh, for the love of—just rise already! It's not that hard!"

I glanced toward the window. Bad idea.

She was leaning over the counter, dark hair tumbling loose around her face, her expression a mix of frustration and determination. And just like that, I was caught.

Something about how she moved—so focused and fierce—made it impossible to look away.

"She's not interested," I muttered under my breath, gathering my tools with a sigh. "And even if she was, she deserves better than me."

That should have been the end of it. It should have been enough to shut it down.

But then she laughed.

And I was laughing too, against my better judgment—against everything I told myself.

***

OLIVIA

I stood on my tiptoes, stretching as far as I could, fingers grazing the bottle of white cooking wine on the highest shelf. Almost. Almost. I pushed up even higher with a determined huff, refusing to admit defeat.

"Vertically challenged?"

Jack's voice startled me so badly that I nearly knocked the bottle off the shelf. My grip on the wood tightened as I spun around, heart pounding, to find him leaning casually against the pantry doorframe, his dirt-smudged t-shirt clinging to broad shoulders.

Unfair.

"I'm managing just fine," I said, wobbling slightly as I reached again, still too stubborn to use the step stool sitting literally three feet away.

Jack pushed off the doorframe and stepped into the pantry, instantly shrinking the space. He didn't hesitate; he just reached up and grabbed the bottle like it was nothing, holding it out with an infuriating smirk.

"Here you go, shorty."

I snatched it from his hand, but the moment our fingers brushed, something unexpected flickered in his expression. The teasing in his eyes softened—just a fraction—but enough to make my pulse stutter.

"Thanks," I murmured, suddenly hyperaware of his scent—soap, fresh air, and something undeniably him.

"You're welcome," he said, his voice quieter now. His gaze lingered longer than it should have, enough to make my stomach dip.

I cleared my throat, gripping the bottle tighter. Focus, Olivia. "Shouldn't you be fixing something?"

Jack shrugged, leaning against the doorframe again. "Fence is done. Gate latch, too. I even fixed the lock on the guesthouse so it doesn't stick anymore."

"Oh." I scrambled for something else to say, my thoughts suddenly useless. "Well, I'm sure there's something else to keep you busy."

He smirked. "Probably. But I thought I'd check to see if you needed anything first."

His words were innocent enough, but the way his voice dipped slightly on *you* sent a flutter through my chest that I absolutely refused to acknowledge.

My lips parted, but for once, no witty retort came to mind.

Jack tilted his head slightly, his grin softening. "Olivia?"

I blinked, snapping out of whatever ridiculous daze I'd fallen into. "I'm fine," I said quickly, stepping back—only to bump straight into the shelf behind me.

Smooth.

Jack chuckled, and its warmth curled around me like a lazy ember. "Anytime," he said, pausing briefly before turning to leave.

I should have let him go.

But I didn't.

"Jack?"

He turned, raising an eyebrow.

I opened my mouth, immediately regretting the words tumbling out. "Would you maybe want to join me for dinner?"

The second I said it, I wanted to snatch it back, rewrite the moment, pretend I hadn't just invited him to sit across from me and make things more complicated.

But then he smiled. Not his usual cocky smirk—something real. Warm. Genuine.

"Yeah," he said, his voice steady, sure. "I'd really like that."

My stomach flipped. "Okay, good," I said, forcing myself to sound normal. "Seven?"

"Seven sounds perfect."

Our eyes met for just a beat too long before he turned and walked away, leaving me standing in the pantry wondering what the hell I'd just done.

What in the name of all things rational had possessed me to ask that?

I should've just let him walk out of here with his smug smile and ridiculous ability to reach high places. Instead, I'd blurted out an invitation like a nervous teenager, and now I was having dinner with him.

My brain caught up a second too late, listing off all the reasons this was a bad idea:

1. Jack was Jack. Too charming, too confident, too good at throwing me off balance.

2. Jack was temporarily living in my guesthouse. Which meant there'd be no escaping him if this turned awkward.

3. Jack made my pulse do stupid, fluttery things it had no business doing.

I exhaled sharply, trying to calm my stomach's ridiculous swirl of nerves. It was just dinner. No big deal.

Right?

Biscuit sauntered into the pantry, tail flicking as if he could sense my impending meltdown. He sat primly at my feet and gave me a look.

"Oh, don't start," I muttered, rubbing my temples. "It's just one meal. It doesn't mean anything."

Biscuit blinked slowly. Judging me.

I groaned. I was officially losing my mind.

Shaking off my nerves, I squared my shoulders and entered the kitchen.

I could handle this.

Probably.

Chapter Four

♥

OLIVIA

The kitchen was warm with the scent of rosemary and garlic, the kind of aroma that made me hopeful I hadn't just wasted an entire afternoon. I pulled the bubbling dish from the oven, setting it on the counter with a critical eye. It *looked* perfect, but I'd learned the hard way that appearances could be deceiving.

Jack's voice broke through my thoughts before I even saw him. "Something smells amazing."

I turned to find him leaning in the doorway, freshly showered, his damp hair still mussed, a clean shirt stretched across his broad chest.

"Thanks," I said, setting the dish down. Jack raised an eyebrow, and I sighed. "You helped with the fence and the gate. I figured I'd feed you as a thank you."

"Generous of you," he said, dropping into a chair. "But this feels suspiciously like a setup."

I smirked, grabbing a spatula. "It is. You're my guinea pig. I've been working on this recipe for a while, but this is the first time I've tested it on an actual human."

Jack leaned back, eyeing me with amused suspicion. "So there's a chance I won't survive this?"

"Pretty much." I plated a serving and set it in front of him. "But hey, if it works, I'll name the dish after you."

Jack stared down at his plate, the rich sauce glistening over perfectly cooked chicken—at least, I *hoped* it was perfectly cooked. He poked it cautiously with his fork. "Should I ask what's in it, or is it safer if I don't know?"

"Chicken, cream sauce, Dijon, rosemary, a lot of garlic... and love," I deadpanned, arms crossing as I watched him.

Jack arched an eyebrow. "Love, huh? Sounds dangerous."

"Just eat it, Lawson."

Still skeptical, he cut into the chicken and took a bite. I watched, waiting for some kind of reaction. He chewed slowly, then froze.

I leaned in, narrowing my eyes. "What? Too garlicky? Too creamy? Be honest, I can take it."

Jack set his fork down and looked at me with an unreadable expression. "Olivia... this might be the best thing I've ever tasted."

I frowned. "You're messing with me."

"I'm serious." He speared another bite, shaking his head in what looked like genuine awe. "This is *incredible*. If this is your idea of an experiment, sign me up for the next one."

A laugh slipped out before I could stop it, surprising us both. "Okay, okay. I get it. You like it."

"Like it?" Jack shook his head. "If I wasn't already staying in your guesthouse, I'd move in just for this."

I dropped into the chair across from him, shooting him a look of mock warning. "Watch yourself. Sweet talk like that'll get you seconds."

Jack grinned, his blue eyes twinkling with mischief. "All part of my master plan."

***

JACK

I leaned back in my chair, glancing at Olivia as she surveyed the wreckage of our meal—plates practically licked clean, not a bite left untouched. Yeah, this recipe was a keeper. And judging by the way her lips curled ever so slightly, she knew it too.

"So," I said, breaking the easy silence, "how long have you been in Anchor Bay?"

"About a year and a half," she said, twisting her wine glass between her fingers. "Came here when my restaurant closed. Figured this town was quiet enough to start over without anyone asking questions."

That caught my attention. I raised an eyebrow. "Asking questions?"

She laughed softly, staring at the tablecloth like it might have answers. "Nothing dramatic. I just needed a fresh start. Somewhere, I could be more than the chef who lost everything... a failure, you know?"

That word landed like a punch to the gut. "Failure?" I frowned. "I can't picture you failing at anything."

She let out a hollow chuckle. "Then you've got a great imagination. I thought I had it all figured out—found a business partner, built something great—until I realized they were a fraud. By the time I caught wind of their con game, everything went straight to hell. The restaurant crashed and burned, my bank account flatlined, and I hit a low I didn't even know existed."

Heat crawled up my chest, raw anger taking hold. Someone had played Olivia for a fool, and that thought lit a fire I couldn't stamp out. I clenched my jaw, trying to keep cool. "That's beyond messed up. But hey, Olivia, getting back up when life knocks you down? That's not failure. That's strength."

Her eyes found mine, a flicker of vulnerability crossing her face. "Thanks," she said softly. "Life's been a mess lately, but here, something just clicks."

"Yeah?" I shifted closer, drawn in by her rare candor. "What makes it special?"

She hesitated, and then her lips curved up. "The quiet."

"The quiet?"

"First time in forever, I feel like I can actually think," she said. With a hint of mischief, she added, "And hey, the locals aren't half bad."

I laughed. "High praise."

She shifted, flipping the script. "Your turn. You seem like you've got roots here in Anchor Bay. How long have you been here?"

"Five years or so," I said, absently tracing the table's edge with my thumb. "Moved here after—" My voice caught, shoulders going rigid before I made myself relax. "After a call went sideways."

Her face softened with interest. "A call?"

"House fire," I said, my voice quieter now. "Did everything I could, but I couldn't save everyone. First time I lost someone on the job." I swallowed hard, forcing the memory back where it belonged. "That kind of thing stays with you." I shook my head, exhaling. "I thought moving to a smaller town and slowing things down would help. But running away doesn't fix everything."

Her eyes softened. "I'm so sorry, Jack. I wish I knew what to say."

Her fingers brushed over mine across the table. Such a simple touch, but it knocked the wind out of me.

I looked up, meeting her eyes. "Something's different here, though. These people - this team - they're the real deal. For the first time in ages, I feel like I'm not just spinning my wheels."

Her eyes locked with mine, her face unreadable. "Isn't it strange?" she said quietly. "Both of us winding up here, looking for a fresh start."

I exhaled slowly, managing a half-smile. "Yeah, we did. Life's got a weird sense of humor."

"Yeah," she murmured, the ghost of a smile playing at her lips. "Funny."

The air between us shifted, thickening with something neither of us spoke aloud. The kitchen suddenly felt smaller, the space between us nonexistent. Olivia's green eyes stayed locked on mine, and for a second, I thought maybe, just maybe—but then Olivia cleared her throat and leaned back, breaking the moment.

"Thanks for dinner," I said, my voice lower than expected. "And for trusting me enough to let me be your guinea pig."

Her lips parted, her fingers still curled around her wine glass. "Anytime," she said, and I could see she was retreating. I could see it in how she grabbed the dishes, turning to busy herself like the simple task could erase whatever had just passed between us.

"Let me help with those," I said, my voice low, steady.

She startled, nearly dropping the glass in her hands. "I'm fine," she said quickly, but the slight tremble in her voice told a different story.

A quiet chuckle slipped from me. "Always so independent," I mused. "Letting someone lend a hand occasionally wouldn't kill you."

She turned, and suddenly, we were closer than I expected, closer than I probably should have let happen. Her green eyes flicked up to mine, wary yet curious, and for a second, I forgot every reason I'd told myself to keep my distance.

"I'm not used to it," she murmured, gaze dropping to the floor.

"I know," I said, softer now, watching her.

She flinched subtly when my fingers brushed against her arm—a light touch meant to reassure, not push. I expected her to pull away. Instead, she stayed rooted to the spot, the space between us growing smaller by the second.

"Olivia," I said, her name rough on my tongue, heavy with something I hadn't meant to say out loud. "I know you're not looking for anything. And I'm not trying to make this complicated. But I can't get you out of my head."

Her breath caught, and her fingers curled tighter around the dish towel.

I should have stepped back, given her space to pretend this moment never happened. Instead, I found myself leaning in, slow enough that she had every chance to stop me.

But she didn't.

She tilted her face up, drawn toward me the same way I was drawn to her. Like gravity. Like inevitability.

***

OLIVIA

I traced my fingers up Jack's chest while he cradled my face, kissing me with an intensity that left me unsteady. I sank into him, my body flush against his sturdy frame as his hands found my hips, eliminating what little space remained between us. Jack pressed me against the counter, effortlessly lifting me to sit on the edge. I wrapped my legs around his waist, pulling him closer as he kissed his way down my neck.

"Jack," I gasped, tilting my head to give him better access. His stubble scraped deliciously against my sensitive skin. He pulled back slightly, his blue eyes dark with want. "Tell me to stop," he murmured, his voice rough. "If this isn't what you want…"

My pulse quickened as I met Jack's piercing blue stare. My mind raced with warning signals—this wasn't part of the plan. He was meant to be passing through, not making me question everything. But a small, traitorous voice in the back of my mind whispered that this was precisely what I wanted. And the way he looked at me, the feel of his muscular body pressed against mine, made it impossible to think clearly.

"I don't want you to stop," I whispered, trembling slightly. Jack's eyes darkened further at my words. He cupped my face gently in his hands, his thumbs caressing my cheeks. "Are you sure?" he asked softly. "Because once we start this, I don't think I'll be able to let you go."

Instead of answering, I pulled him in for another searing kiss. Jack's hand slid slowly up my thigh, pushing the fabric of my skirt higher as he went. His calloused fingers left trails of heat on my sensitive skin. My breath hitched as Jack's hand inched ever upward, his touch gentle and insistent.

The kitchen faded away around us as Jack's fingers traced delicate patterns on the inside of my thigh. My skin tingled everywhere he touched me. I parted my legs, silently urging him on. Jack's hand moved higher still, his fingertips finally brushing against the lace edge of my panties.

I gasped softly, my hips instinctively rocking forward to meet his touch. Jack groaned low in his throat, his forehead resting against mine as his fingers explored the damp fabric. He stroked me through the thin lace, his touch feather-light.

"Is this okay?" Jack whispered, his breath warm and teasing against my skin. I could only nod, words failing me as his fingers traced upward, brushing my clit through the delicate lace of my underwear. I whimpered, my legs falling open wider in invitation. Jack groaned low in his throat. His thumb brushed over my panties, feeling the dampness that had soaked through the thin fabric.

"God, you're so wet," he growled, his voice husky with desire. I gasped as Jack slipped his fingers beneath the lace, finally touching my bare skin. He stroked me slowly, exploring my folds with reverent care. When his thumb found my clit, I cried out softly, my hips bucking against his hand.

"Jack," I whimpered, gripping his broad shoulders. He captured my lips in a kiss as he slid one finger inside me. I cried out at the sensation, my inner walls clenching around him. Jack added a second finger, curling them to hit that perfect spot inside me. His thumb circled my clit as he pumped his fingers in and out.

I was lost in sensation, waves of pleasure building with each stroke of Jack's skilled fingers. I rocked against his hand, chasing my release. Jack's lips trailed hot kisses down my neck as he quickened his pace.

I threw my head back, overwhelmed by the sensation. Jack's fingers moved faster, his thumb still working my clit. I could feel myself climbing higher, hovering on the edge of bliss. Jack's lips found my ear, his voice low and rough. "Let go, Olivia. I've got you."

His words pushed me over the edge, and I cried out as pleasure crashed over me. Jack held me close, his fingers slowing as he eased me through the aftershocks.

When I finally caught my breath, my eyes fluttered open to find Jack's intense gaze fixed on me. With deliberate slowness, he pulled his hand away and brought his wet fingers to his mouth. I couldn't help but stare as he tasted them, his dark eyes locked with mine the entire time.

"Jack, I need you," I panted, my voice barely a whisper.

"Say it again," Jack rasped, his voice thick with desire.

"I... I need you," I repeated, boldly meeting his intense gaze.

"Olivia—"

The shrill ring of my phone sliced through the moment, yanking me back to reality. My stomach dropped. Not now.

Jack let out a frustrated groan, dragging a hand through his hair. "You've got to be kidding."

I ignored him, reaching for my phone. The second I saw the name on the screen, my heart squeezed. "It's Theo."

Jack's eyes narrowed. "Theo?"

"A friend," I said quickly, pressing the phone to my ear. "Theo, hey. What's going on?"

Theo's voice was tight, bordering on frantic.

"Wait, what?" I swung my legs off the counter, straightening my dress as I paced. "Theo, slow down. What happened?"

Jack stepped closer, watching me as I pressed my fingers to my temple, trying to piece together what Theo was saying.

"No, it's okay. Are you hurt? ... Okay. Did you call the police?"

Jack stiffened at that, his brows drawing together.

"I'm coming now," I said, my voice firm. "Fifteen minutes tops. Try to stay calm."

I ended the call and turned, only to find Jack standing there, arms crossed, expression unreadable.

"What's wrong?" His voice was steady, but I caught the tension beneath it.

I inhaled deeply, trying to steady the adrenaline racing through me. "Someone trashed Theo's bar. Smashed windows and broken bottles—basically destroyed the place. The police are there, but he's a mess. Asked if I could come."

Jack's jaw ticked. "The Rusty Anchor?"

I nodded, shoving my feet into my shoes. "Yeah. That bar is his whole life. He really didn't need this right now."

Jack exhaled sharply. "You're going alone?"

I glanced up. "Of course. Why?"

"It's late." He stepped forward, his voice low, measured. "Whoever did this might still be around. I'm coming with you."

I blinked. "Jack, I appreciate it, but you don't have to. The cops are there, and really... Theo just needs a friend right now."

His gaze held mine, searching. "I get that. But Anchor Bay or not, you don't know who did this. I'd feel better if you weren't going alone."

I tilted my head, giving him a small smile. "Jack, I get that you're worried, but trust me. I've managed just fine on my own for years."

His expression shuttered, arms folding tighter across his chest. "Right. Message received. Heaven forbid anyone actually wants to help you."

His words hit like a slap, knocking the air from my lungs.

I softened. "I know you're trying to help," I said carefully. "But Theo... he's been my rock since I first came to Anchor Bay. When everything felt impossible, he was there for me. I owe him this."

Jack's throat bobbed. "You're right. You can handle yourself. I just—" He exhaled, dragging a hand through his hair. "I care about you, Olivia. Can't help but worry when you might be walking into trouble."

The weight of his words settled deep, pressing into something I wasn't ready to face.

"I know, Jack," I murmured. "I do. But Theo needs me right now, and I can't turn my back on that."

Jack sighed, the fight draining from his shoulders. "Yeah. Fine. Go help your friend. Just... watch yourself, okay?"

I grabbed my keys and headed for the door, but before stepping outside, I glanced back.

"Thanks for caring, Jack," I whispered. Then I walked out into the night.

Chapter Five

♥

JACK

After Olivia left, I paced the kitchen, raking a hand through my hair. The easy flow of conversation we'd had earlier was gone, replaced by a tight, nagging knot in my gut. I knew Olivia could handle herself, but that didn't change how I felt. I wanted to be there. To protect her. Hell, if I was being honest, I wanted her to need me.

Exhaustion tugged at me, but sleep wasn't happening. I dropped onto the couch, staring at the ceiling, my thoughts circling Theo like a vulture on a fresh carcass. Olivia had called him her oldest friend in Anchor Bay, but the way she'd bolted the second he called didn't sit right. There was something more there—I just didn't know what.

Eventually, I dragged myself to the guesthouse, but the rest still wouldn't come. My mind wouldn't stop picturing Olivia curled up on Theo's couch, his arm draped around her, their heads bent close as they whispered through the night. It was stupid. Olivia had said they were just friends. But was that how Theo saw it?

I squeezed my eyes shut, willing sleep to take over. It didn't.

By the time the sky started to lighten, I'd given up. I shuffled to the tiny kitchenette, brewing a pot of coffee strong enough to wake the dead. It did nothing to chase away the tension coiled in my chest.

I paced, the hours crawling by. A third cup of coffee sat cold and untouched on the counter. The longer I went without a word from Olivia, the tighter my frustration wound.

Then, finally, I heard the crunch of tires in the driveway. I was already out the door before she even had a chance to cut the engine.

She stepped out, looking drained, her hair mussed, her clothes rumpled. I barely registered the dried streaks of tears on her cheeks before frustration overrode concern.

"Where the hell have you been?" The words came out harsher than I intended, but I didn't care.

Olivia blinked at me, startled. "I told you. I was with Theo. His bar—"

I ran a hand through my hair, every muscle in my body tight with frustration. "Do you have any idea how worried I've been?"

Her eyes flashed with irritation. "Worried? Jack, I told you where I was going. Theo needed me. His bar was trashed, he was a mess—"

"All night?" I cut in, unable to hold back the edge in my voice. "What could possibly take that long?"

Her brows pulled together, her own frustration rising to meet mine. "We were dealing with the police, talking to his insurance company, cleaning up what we could. It was a mess, Jack." She crossed her arms, her jaw set. "I didn't realize I needed your permission to help a friend. Theo was devastated. I wasn't about to leave him alone."

"Right," I scoffed. "Because Theo's the only one who matters."

Her spine stiffened. "What exactly are you getting at?"

I let out a bitter laugh, shaking my head. "The minute Theo calls, you race out of here like his personal savior. Meanwhile, I'm left here wondering if something happened to you."

"That's not how it is," Olivia shot back. "His bar was destroyed. He was a mess. What was I supposed to do, ignore him?"

"Here's a wild thought," I said, jaw tight, "maybe call the one person who literally offered to help?"

I clenched my jaw, my hands fisting at my sides. I had no right to be angry. But damn it, I was. And the worst part? It wasn't just about Theo. It was about how easy it was for Olivia to let someone else in—someone who wasn't me.

***

OLIVIA

My eyes narrowed as I pinned Jack with a glare. "Called you? Jack, I don't even have your number. And honestly, I don't appreciate what you're implying." My voice was sharp, but my heart pounded, my emotions raw from the long night. "Theo is my friend, nothing more. And even if he was, it's none of your business. You and me, we're not... we're not anything, Jack. You don't get to question where I spend my time or who I spend it with."

His jaw tightened, frustration and something else—hurt?—flashing in his expression. "Right. We're not anything. Just two people who almost..." He trailed off, running a rough hand through his hair. "I get it. I'm just the guy crashing in your guesthouse. I don't have any right to worry about you or care where you've been all night."

The pain in his voice made my anger flicker, but I couldn't let it soften me. "Jack, you're not listening. When I showed up in Anchor Bay, I was lost. No direction, no hope—nothing. Theo didn't just give me a job; he gave me a chance when I needed it most. He was the first person here who actually saw me. So yeah, when he needs help, I will be there."

Jack's jaw remained tight, but something in his eyes wavered. I could see the reluctant understanding there, even if he wasn't ready to accept it. He exhaled sharply, dragging a hand through his hair again. "Forget it."

He stepped back, his hands falling to his sides, his shoulders still tight with tension. "I need to get to the station," he said abruptly.

I blinked. "Right now?"

"Yeah," he muttered, not quite meeting my gaze. "Got a shift."

I opened my mouth, but no words came. The weight of everything we hadn't said hung heavy between us.

"Jack," I said, my voice quieter now.

He turned, his expression guarded but not unkind. "Olivia, it's fine. Really."

"It doesn't feel fine," I admitted, stepping toward him. "Look, I know things got heated, but I—"

"Don't." Jack held up a hand, his voice calm but firm. "You don't owe me an explanation. You don't owe me anything."

Frustration sparked in my chest. "That's not what I—"

"I get it," he said, cutting me off gently. His voice was quieter now, tinged with something final. "Theo's your friend. You were there for him, just like you should've been. And I'm... I'm just the guy staying in your guesthouse. End of story."

I inhaled sharply, searching for something—anything—to fix whatever had just broken between us. But before I could find the words, Jack gave a short nod and turned toward his truck, his boots crunching against the gravel.

"Be safe," I murmured, more to myself than to him.

Jack paused with his hand on the door, glancing back at me. Something passed between us for a second—maybe regret or something heavier. Then he was gone.

The silence he left behind felt deafening. Wrapping my arms around myself, I stood there, staring at the empty driveway, the argument replaying in my head. My chest felt tight, but I didn't know if it was from anger or something worse.

Things between us had unraveled so quickly, and I had no idea how to pull them back together.

Chapter Six

♥

JACK

The firehouse buzzed with the usual energy—radio static humming in the background, the murmur of voices blending with the distant clang of equipment, and the ever-present scent of stale coffee lingering in the air. I sat at the long table in the common area, staring at the mug before me, my fingers tapping restlessly against the ceramic.

I'd come in hoping work would clear my head, that routine would drown out the conversation still looping through my mind. But Olivia's words refused to fade, sharp and soft simultaneously, needling at my chest with every replay.

Boots scuffed against the tile floor, pulling my attention. Glancing up, I spotted Brooke Taylor, one of Anchor Bay's patrol officers, standing near the doorway, chatting with one of the guys. Clipboard in hand, her dark blonde ponytail swayed as she gestured animatedly.

Pushing away from the table, I strode toward her. "Brooke."

She turned, giving me a curious once-over. "Lawson. What's up?"

I slouched against the doorframe, hands stuffed in my pockets to hide their fidgeting. "Hey, got anything new on the Rusty Anchor case?"

Her eyebrow shot up. "You know Theo?"

I kept my voice casual, aiming for indifference. "No, not really. Word got around about the break-in. Thought you might have a lead."

Brooke's face relaxed slightly. "Total disaster zone in there. Broken windows and trashed furniture, subtle wasn't their style. We're following a few leads, but between you and me—these weren't exactly professionals."

I tried to focus on the details of the case but couldn't help myself. "How's Theo taking it?"

Brooke's smile turned, knowing in a way that made me want to bolt. "Honestly? Better than expected. Olivia Harper showed up right after it happened. And, well... Theo's not the type to let people in, but he lets her help."

Something clenched in my gut. "Good for him," I muttered, my voice tighter than I meant for it to be.

Brooke studied me for a second, then cocked her head. "Look, Jack... I don't know what's going on with you, and it's really none of my business. But I can tell Olivia and Theo spending time together is getting under your skin."

I went still. "I don't know what you're talking about."

She let out a dry laugh. "Right. Sure you don't." Crossing her arms, she leaned slightly against the wall. "If it helps, they're just friends. Theo and Olivia clicked when she moved here, but that's all it's ever been. She was there for him when he needed it, and he's been a good friend to her. That's it."

I nodded slowly, the tension in my chest easing a fraction, but Brooke wasn't blind—she caught the flicker of relief in my face, and her lips curved slightly.

"Theo's a good guy, by the way," she added.

Something in the way she said it made me pause. "You and Theo?"

Her expression softened, and she gave a slight nod. "Yeah. We've been dancing around it for a while, but... yeah, I like him."

It hit me like a punch to the gut. All this time, I'd been stewing over nothing. Doubting Olivia. Letting my insecurities build up a wall between us when she hadn't given me a single reason not to trust her.

Jesus. I was an idiot.

Brooke must've seen something shift in my expression because she quirked a brow. "You okay?"

I exhaled, dragging a hand through my hair. "Just realized I screwed up. Badly."

She smirked. "Yeah, I got that." But she didn't push. Instead, she straightened, tucking her clipboard under her arm. "Hope you figure it out. And let me know if you hear anything about the break-in."

"Will do," I said, my voice quieter now. "Thanks, Brooke."

She gave me a small wave and walked off, leaving me standing in the doorway, hands on my hips, staring after her.

I let out a slow breath. Olivia had told me the truth, and I hadn't listened. Instead, I'd let my own baggage turn me into the kind of guy I never wanted to be—one who pushed people away because he was too damn scared of not being enough.

You're better than this, Lawson. And she deserves better than what you gave her.

I slumped back toward the table, where my coffee sat cold and untouched, mocking the hours I'd wasted wallowing in my own idiocy. Knowing I'd screwed up wasn't going to cut it.

I had to make this right.

***

My hands clenched the steering wheel as I stared at Olivia's kitchen window, warm light flooding into the darkness. She was definitely awake. The hint of cinnamon in the air told me she was probably baking.

I let out a long breath, my heart pounding against my ribs. Enough running. Enough letting these stupid doubts run the show. Time to face her and fix what I broke.

I hauled myself out of the truck, forcing my feet up the porch steps. At her door, I paused long enough to swallow hard before raising my fist to knock.

Footsteps sounded from inside, and then the door cracked open. Olivia stood there, wearing a flour-covered apron and a wooden spoon gripped in one hand like a makeshift weapon. Her wide green eyes locked onto mine.

"Jack," she said, my name falling between surprise and caution. "What are you doing here?"

I swallowed hard. "I need to talk to you. Can you spare a minute?"

She hesitated for a second and I thought she might tell me to get lost. But then she stepped back, wordlessly letting me in.

The scent of sugar and spices wrapped around me as I followed her to the kitchen. The place was a disaster—flour dusted nearly every surface, mixing bowls were scattered across the counters, and the sink overflowed with dishes. It was chaos, but somehow, it felt like her.

"I'm in the middle of something," she said, tossing the wooden spoon onto the counter and crossing her arms. "So whatever this is, make it quick."

I met her eyes, steady despite the knot in my chest. "I was wrong this morning," I admitted. "I should have believed you. I should have trusted you. And I'm sorry."

Her expression flickered, something unreadable crossing her face before she pulled her arms tighter around herself. "Jack, don't—"

"Let me finish," I cut in gently. "I messed up. My own insecurities got in the way, and I made assumptions about you and Theo because I couldn't handle being jealous. That's on me, not you."

She searched my face, her stance stiff but uncertain. "Jealous?"

I let out a dry laugh, raking a hand through my hair. "Yeah. I know what you said, and I believe you. But last night, waiting and wondering, I started questioning everything. And my feelings got tangled up."

Her breath hitched, just barely, but I caught it.

"What feelings?" she asked quietly.

I stepped closer, close enough to catch the faint scent of vanilla clinging to her skin. "Olivia," I murmured, my voice rough. "I care about you. More than I expected. More than I know how to handle if I'm being honest. And the thought of you running off to be with someone else, even just as a friend, it—" I exhaled sharply, shaking my head. "It messed with my head."

She stared at me, her arms falling to her sides, tension draining from her frame. "Jack..."

"Wait," I said before she could cut me off. "I know I screwed up. I should have trusted you instead of acting like a damn fool. I'm not the jealous type but with you..." I let out a breathless laugh, meeting her eyes. "Apparently, I don't have a clue how to be anything else."

***

OLIVIA

"I like you too, Jack," I admitted softly, my voice barely above a whisper. "And that scares me."

He stepped closer, close enough that I could feel his warmth. "Why does it scare you?"

I swallowed hard, dropping my gaze momentarily before meeting his eyes again. "Because I've been hurt before," I confessed. "I came to Anchor Bay to start over, focus on my career, and avoid getting tangled up in anything messy. And then you showed up and..." I trailed off, shaking my head.

Jack reached out, his fingers brushing against my cheek before he tucked a loose strand of hair behind my ear. "And what?" he asked, his voice softer now.

"And you made me want things I thought I'd given up on," I admitted, my voice barely above a whisper.

Jack cupped my face, his hands warm and gentle, his touch grounding me. "Olivia," he murmured. "I'm right here. Whatever's scaring you—you don't have to do it alone."

A sharp breath hitched in my throat at the tenderness in his voice. His thumb traced along my cheek, and when our eyes met, there was nothing but sincerity in his gaze.

"Jack," I whispered, my voice trembling. "I'm scared of how much I want this... want you."

He leaned in until his forehead rested against mine. "I'm scared too," he admitted, his breath fanning against my lips. "But this thing between us? It's worth the risk."

I pressed my palms against his chest, his heartbeat steady and strong beneath my touch. His warmth seeped into me, melting away traces of fear I didn't know still lingered. Everything else disappeared when Jack leaned in, his lips barely grazing mine, awakening something I'd kept buried. The kiss began tentatively, testing, but that gentleness didn't last. Heat flared between us, my arms winding around his neck as he pulled me in, pressing me flush against him.

"Olivia," he murmured against my skin, his voice thick with something raw, something dangerous. "I want you so much."

"I want you too," I breathed, my fingers threading into his hair, tugging slightly as a shiver ran through me.

Our breaths mingled, hearts hammering in sync. Jack pressed his forehead to mine again, his hands framing my face like he feared I might disappear.

"Maybe we should—" he started, his voice low and rough.

"Yes," I answered before he could finish, the single word trembling quickly from my lips. My fingers laced with his as I stepped back, pulling him with me toward the bedroom.

Chapter Seven

♥

OLIVIA

I heard Jack murmur against my neck, "God, Olivia, you're intoxicating," his warm breath sent shivers along my skin. Heat rushed through me at his touch as his fingers moved deliberately down my blouse until the fabric slipped away to reveal my red lace bra. I felt his fingertips skim the delicate patterns. At the same time, his dark eyes followed every move, and I shivered under his intense gaze, my body responding instantly as my nipples tightened beneath the thin material.

My senses were overwhelmed by Jack. There was just so much of him. His smell intoxicated me, and his warm, calloused hands and probing tongue sent me reeling. The men I was used to dating were not working men. They were mainly professionals and were not heavily muscled, nor were their hands calloused. In some instances, their hands had been even softer than mine. I had never considered this a problem before, but feeling Jack's rough hands move across my breasts to tease my nipples, I realized how much more pleasurable this was.

With slow, deliberate movements, Jack unhooked my bra and took each nipple into his mouth, swirling his tongue around the sensitive buds. I whimpered and pressed my fingers against his shoulders, my body trembling with each wave of pleasure that rushed through me as I surrendered completely to the sensation.

Jack eased me back onto the thick mattress before moving over me, his eyes drinking in every detail of my bare skin. His fingers traced lazy patterns down my sides, along the gentle curve of my waist, leading to the waistband of my jeans. My breath hitched as his hands lingered there, teasing at the button.

With agonizing slowness, Jack undid the button and eased down the zipper. I lifted my hips to let him slide the denim down my legs. His touch left trails of fire along my skin as he peeled away the fabric, revealing inch by inch of my smooth thighs.

Jack's breath caught when he saw my red lacy underwear—a perfect match to the bra left forgotten on the floor. His thumbs found the edge of the delicate lace and tugged downward with deliberate slowness. The fabric caught for a moment against my wetness, silently affirming just how much I wanted him.

***

JACK

I laid Olivia back on the bed and moved my attention to her nipples. They were rosy pink, and I almost lost it right there, just looking at them. I had never been with a woman who turned me on the way

Olivia turned me on. I needed to keep my wits about me to ensure she reached climax before I did.

I pushed her breasts together and took both of her nipples into my mouth simultaneously. I sucked on them while winding my tongue around and between them. Arching back, Olivia cried out in pleasure, tangling her hands in the bedsheets.

As I worked on her nipples, I felt one of her hands slide down between us. I wasn't ready for her to touch me yet, so I pulled my hips back just out of her reach. To my surprise, she then rerouted her hand to her own wet curls, slipping inside, searching for her clit.

"No, you don't," I chuckled hoarsely. "It isn't time for that yet, you little minx." Guiding her hand away, I started to move down her body, kissing and licking my way down to her pussy. I positioned her legs over my shoulders and inhaled deeply, holding myself steady just an inch away from her exposed clit.

I could feel Olivia's thighs quivering against my shoulders as I hovered tantalizingly close to her most sensitive spot. Reaching up to pluck at her nipples, I lowered my mouth closer to her clit. Her scent was intoxicating, tangy, and sweet, and I felt ready to explode. I couldn't resist any longer.

"Please," Olivia whispered, her voice thick with desire.

With deliberate slowness, I ran my tongue along her slick folds, savoring her taste. Olivia's sharp intake of breath and the way her hips bucked upward told me everything I needed to know. I gripped her thighs firmly, holding her in place as I explored every inch of her with my mouth.

My tongue circled her clit, teasing but never quite giving her the direct contact she craved. Olivia's fingers threaded through my hair, tugging gently as she tried to guide me where she wanted me most. I resisted, continuing my torturously slow pace.

I alternated between long, languid strokes and quick, teasing flicks, feeling Olivia's body responding to every movement. Her breathy moans filled the room, spurring me on. I could feel her getting closer, her thighs tensing around my head.

I slipped two fingers inside her, curling them upward to find that sensitive spot. Olivia cried out, her back arching off the bed. I sucked her clit between my lips, applying firm pressure as I pumped my fingers in and out.

"Jack, oh God, Jack," Olivia panted, her hips rocking against my face.

I could feel her inner walls starting to flutter around my fingers. Determined to push her over the edge, I increased my pace, my tongue moving in quick circles over her swollen clit.

Olivia's body went rigid, a strangled cry escaping her lips as her orgasm crashed over her. I held her steady, my mouth still working against her as wave after wave of pleasure coursed through her body. Her thighs trembled against my shoulders, her fingers gripping my hair almost painfully as she rode out the intense sensations.

As Olivia's climax began to subside, I gentled my movements, placing soft kisses along her inner thighs. Her chest heaved as she caught her breath, a light sheen of sweat glistening on her flushed skin.

I climbed up to meet her lips in a fierce kiss. Olivia's taste lingered on my tongue, fueling our desire. Her nails traced fire down my back, drawing me nearer.

"Jack," Olivia whispered against my lips. "I need you. Please."

I braced myself over her, muscles tight with restraint. I struggled to maintain control, but her hand sliding down and caressing my erection through my pants shattered any restraint I had left. A low moan escaped my lips as she began to stroke me, her touch igniting sparks of pleasure throughout my body.

Olivia's nimble fingers worked at my belt buckle, her touch sending shivers down my spine. I helped her slide my pants down, kicking them off impatiently. My boxers strained against my throbbing erection, a damp spot forming where the tip pressed against the fabric.

Olivia hooked her fingers under the waistband, slowly dragging my underwear down. My cock sprang free, hard and aching for her touch. Olivia's eyes darkened with lust as she took in the sight of me fully naked.

I fumbled in my discarded pants pocket, fishing out a foil packet with trembling hands. I tore it open carefully, rolling the condom down my length. The sensation made me twitch, and I had to take a deep breath to center myself.

Olivia guided me toward her entrance, and we moaned as I entered her. I took a moment to savor the sensation before I began to move.

I slowly pushed deeper into Olivia, savoring every exquisite inch as her warmth enveloped me. Her legs wrapped around my waist, pulling me closer, urging me deeper. I braced my forearms on either side of her head, my eyes locked on hers as I began to move.

Our bodies found a rhythm, slow and sensual at first. Olivia's hips rose to meet each of my thrusts, taking me in completely. I dipped my head to capture her lips in a searing kiss, swallowing her soft moans of pleasure.

"You feel incredible," I murmured against her neck, trailing kisses along her collarbone. The scent of her skin, a mix of perfume and desire, filled my senses.

She responded by arching her back and pressing her breasts against my chest. I could feel her hardened nipples grazing my skin, sending jolts of electricity through my body. I slid a hand between us, my fingers finding her still-sensitive clit. I circled it gently, matching the rhythm of my thrusts. Olivia gasped, her nails digging into my shoulders.

"Oh God, Jack," she panted, her voice thick with desire. "Faster, please, harder."

I obliged, picking up the pace. The room filled with the sound of our labored breathing and the slap of skin on skin. Olivia's hands roamed my back, tracing the contours of my muscles as they flexed with each movement.

I could feel the tension building in my core, a familiar tightening that signaled I was close. But I was determined to bring Olivia over the edge again before I let go. I angled my hips, hitting that spot deep inside her that made her cry out in ecstasy.

"Come for me, Olivia," I growled, my voice rough with desire.

Olivia's body responded instantly to my command, her inner walls clenching around me as another orgasm ripped through her. She cried out my name, her back arching off the bed as waves of pleasure coursed through her body. The sight of her coming undone beneath me, combined with the exquisite pressure of her muscles contracting around my length, pushed me over the edge.

With a guttural groan, I buried myself deep inside her as my own release hit. My vision blurred, every nerve ending in my body singing with pleasure as I pulsed within her. Time seemed to stand still as we clung to each other, our bodies trembling in the aftermath of our shared ecstasy.

Slowly, our breathing steadied. I carefully withdrew from Olivia, disposing of the condom before collapsing beside her on the bed.

***

OLIVIA

Neither of us spoke for a while, the silence stretching between us comfortably. Just breathing, just existing together. Eventually, Jack shifted, rolling onto his side to face me, propping himself on one elbow.

His eyes swept over me, a lazy smile tugging at his lips as he traced a slow, teasing finger along my arm. "I know this isn't exactly the ideal time for this kind of thing," he said, voice warm and rough, "but I can't hold it in anymore." He hesitated just long enough to make my heart stutter. "Olivia, I love you."

My breath caught, my heart flipping in my chest. Before I could respond, he grinned, the teasing glint in his blue eyes softening the weight of his words.

"And, honestly," he continued, "someone has to keep an eye on you in the kitchen. I'd hate to think what would happen if you didn't have me around to rescue you from another fire."

I laughed and swatted at his arm, but my eyes stung with unshed tears. "Jack..."

He dipped his head, brushing the softest kiss against my lips before pulling back just enough to hold my gaze. "Marry me, Olivia," he murmured. "Let me spend the rest of my life keeping you safe—whether from kitchen mishaps or anything else that comes our way."

The breath I'd been holding rushed out in a shaky laugh as the tears spilled over. My hands found his face, fingers sliding into his hair, and I looked into those steady, unwavering blue eyes that had somehow become my home.

"Yes," I whispered, my voice thick with emotion. "Yes, Jack. I love you."

His lips found mine again, deep and sure, sealing our promise.

Epilogue

OLIVIA

The warm scent of cinnamon and freshly baked bread filled the air as I adjusted the platter on the farmhouse table. Stepping back, I brushed a smudge of flour from my apron—though plenty was dusted across my hands and, judging by the state of the counter behind me, all over the kitchen. Some things never changed.

"Looks great," Jack said from the doorway, his voice laced with that familiar teasing smirk that still made my heart skip a beat. "Flour and all, Mrs. Lawson."

I turned toward him, grinning as I rested a hand on my slightly rounded belly. "Flour's just part of my charm. You knew what you were signing up for when you married me."

"Absolutely," he said, crossing the room to slide his arms around my waist, pulling me against him. "But don't think I've forgotten I'm on permanent kitchen fire duty."

I laughed, swatting lightly at his chest. "You're never going to let me live that down, are you?"

"Not a chance," he murmured, kissing my forehead.

The sound of voices carried in from the hallway, a mix of laughter and footsteps as friends and family started filtering into the house. Jack stepped back, but not before trailing his fingers along my waist—a casual touch that still sent warmth curling through me.

I took one last look at the table. It wasn't perfect, the kitchen was a mess, and my apron bore the evidence of my work—but as I caught Jack's gaze across the room, my heart swelled.

A little messy, a little chaotic—but absolutely perfect.

***

Dear Reader,

Thank you so much for reading *Sparks of Temptation*! I hope you loved Jack and Olivia's story as much as I loved writing it. Their journey was filled with sparks, laughter, and plenty of heart, and I'm so grateful you came along for the ride.

If you enjoyed the book, I'd truly appreciate it if you took a moment to leave a review. Reviews help authors like me reach more readers, and they mean the world when it comes to sharing these stories. Even a few words can make a huge difference!

Thank you for your support, and I can't wait to share more love stories with you!

With gratitude,Hana York

***

Ready for more?

If you loved *Sparks of Temptation*, you won't want to miss what's coming next! *Love's Anchor* is a swoon-worthy, small-town, friends-to-lovers romance featuring Theo Morgan—a grumpy but charming bar owner whose world is upended when his beloved Rusty Anchor is vandalized—and Brooke Taylor, the no-nonsense cop determined to find the culprit... even if working closely with Theo stirs up feelings she's spent years ignoring.

When an investigation forces them together, old tensions ignite into something neither of them is ready to admit. Will they finally take the risk... or let fear keep them apart?

Keep reading for a sneak peek at Chapter One of *Love's Anchor*!

Sneak Peak of Love's Anchor

♥

THEO

Sunlight streamed through the shattered windows of the Rusty Anchor, throwing long shadows over the wreckage—broken glass, toppled barstools, and the gut-wrenching sight of my once-pristine bar reduced to chaos. My bar. My sanctuary. And some bastard had come in here and wrecked it like it meant nothing. My jaw tightened, fists clenching at my sides. Whoever did this? They were going to pay.

The bell above the door jingled, and my muscles tensed. A sound that usually meant regulars stopping by for a drink now sent a prickle of unease down my spine. I turned to see Brooke Taylor step inside, her badge catching the morning light.

Brooke and I had been friends for years, the kind of friendship built on late-night conversations shared beers, and the unspoken understanding that she always had my back, on and off duty. And I always had hers. She was steady, no-nonsense, and knew me better than most. Lately, though, something had shifted. Maybe it was just me; maybe it was nothing. But standing there, anger still simmering in my chest, my gaze caught on the determined set of her jaw, the sharp focus in her eyes, and for the first time, I wondered—if I reached for her, would she pull away or lean in?

"Morning," she said, her voice calm, cutting through my jumbled thoughts. Her sharp gaze flickered over the destruction, cataloging every detail for the second time. "I couldn't stop thinking about this place last night. Thought I'd stop by and see how you're holding up."

A ghost of a smile tugged at my lips. "Aw, worried about me? I'm touched."

Brooke shot me a flat look. "The bar, Morgan. I'm asking about the bar."

"Ah," I said, letting out a dry laugh. "Total disaster zone. Though I'm considering rebranding—thinking 'artfully distressed' has a nice ring to it."

Brooke arched a brow. "I think 'trashed' is the word you're looking for."

"Nice to see you haven't lost your charm, Officer Taylor," I drawled, crossing my arms.

She took a step closer, flipping open her notepad. "Let's go through this again. Anything new come to mind?"

I exhaled sharply, shaking my head. "Dead end. If I had even a hint of something useful, you'd be slapping cuffs on someone instead of us standing here looking like idiots."

Brooke slumped, letting out a weary sigh. She crouched by the broken window, carefully studying its jagged edges as her ponytail swayed with each slight movement.

She straightened, leveling me with that no-nonsense stare of hers. "Are you going to help me figure this out, or are you planning to stand there brooding all day?"

I smirked. "I can brood and help. I'm nothing if not multi-talented."

For a moment, our eyes locked, and the air shifted—something unspoken crackling between us. It wasn't just the break-in messing with my head. It was her. The way she stood there, determined as ever, acting like she had everything under control when I knew damn well she cared more than she let on. Brooke Taylor could pretend all she wanted, but I could see it—the concern behind her steady gaze, the way she lingered just a little longer than she needed to.

***

Brooke sat at one of the tables in the Rusty Anchor, her notepad open, pen tapping against the wood in a steady rhythm. The sound filled the eerie silence that had taken over the bar—no music, no conversations, just the aftermath of destruction. I stood behind the counter, rearranging bottles that didn't need rearranging, my fingers tightening around the glass as the restless energy inside me refused to settle.

"You're going to wear a groove into that counter," Brooke muttered without looking up.

I paused mid-motion, glancing over at her with a raised brow. "Would you rather I pace? Might add some drama to your 'crime scene'."

She smirked, finally looking up from her notes. "Did anyone stand out last week? Someone acting off, asking weird questions?"

Leaning against the bar, I tried to think back. "Not really. The usual crowd—regulars, tourists stopping in before heading to the bay. Nothing that screamed 'future vandal'."

Brooke jotted something down, her pen moving fast. "What about your staff? Anyone mention seeing someone hanging around after closing?"

I shook my head. "If they did, they didn't tell me. But I'll ask. They're supposed to come by later to help clean up."

"Good," she said, snapping her notebook shut. "I'll need to talk to them too."

I studied her, noticing the tightness in her jaw and the way her fingers tapped against her notepad a little too forcefully. "You're taking this personally," I said, watching for her reaction.

Her gaze flicked up, guarded. "It's my job."

I leaned forward slightly. "It's more than that. You were here within ten minutes of my call last night, Brooke. This feels different."

She held my stare for a beat before sighing, her shoulders dropping slightly. "I hate seeing this happen to you. To the Anchor. It's one of the few places in this town that feels... real. And I don't like seeing people mess with that."

A tightness formed in my chest, something I wasn't ready to unpack. Instead, I forced a lopsided grin. "My knight in shining armor, huh?"

Brooke rolled her eyes, fighting a smile. "Don't flatter yourself. What about security tapes?"

I hesitated, shifting slightly, fingers brushing over my sleeve. "Right. That. The whole system's been glitchy as hell lately. Cameras keep cutting in and out. Been putting off getting it fixed."

Brooke's pen stopped mid-stroke above her notepad. "And this didn't seem worth mentioning earlier because...?"

"Didn't think it was relevant," I admitted, rubbing the back of my neck. "Clearly, I was wrong."

She exhaled slowly, pressing her fingers against her temples like she was trying to will away a headache. "Well, might as well check it out. Maybe we'll get lucky."

I doubted it, but at this point, we could use all the luck we could get.

Love's Anchor **is hitting Amazon February 25, 2025!**